W9-BRI-046

WAR BABY

POETRY
BY
PENNY MCDANIEL-HAYKO

HASOR-PLENNY PUBLISHING
A DIVISION OF PLENNY ENTERPRISES
VALLEY FORGE, PENNSYLVANIA

Published by:

HASOR-PLENNY PUBLISHING
A Division of Plenny Enterprises
Suite 47
1220 Valley Forge Road
P.O. Box 987
Valley Forge, Pennsylvania
19482-0987

Printed in U.S.A.

Copyright © 1996 by Penny McDaniel-Hayko

Library of Congress Catalog Card Number: 96-94604
ISBN: 0-9653811-3-7

A(KNOWLEDGMENTS

The author would like to express her appreciation to the following journals where some of these poems appeared or will appear:

NATURALLY: "The Graveyard"
SOUTH ASH PRESS: "The Game Of Life"
WRITING FOR OUR LIVES: "War Baby"

Cover Design by Penny McDaniel-Hayko and Michael Baklycki.
Cover Art provided by Dover Publications, Inc.

For my husband, Len...
thank you for your love and support.
For Yesenia...
thank you for being you.
For my family and friends...
thank you for the inspiration
and for putting up with me.
And for my Creator...
through whom all things are made possible.

CONTENTS

on being a poet

i am a quiet poet
because i have too much to say

i write
because words scream in silence too

THE GAME OF LIFE

I don't remember having much of a childhood.
Had to earn it over the years. Growing up
wasn't easy, especially after my father split
and mom went to work full-time as a nurse's aide
or something just to put food on the table
for three starving kids,

When I was seven, learning how to cook replaced
playing house with my brother and his imaginary
friend, a magical dragon that was some kind of
super hero;

balancing a checkbook and managing accounts
for my senile, diabetic grandmother
became a real life monopoly game.
I don't play Monopoly anymore.

I remember nights, cramped in the same room
with my brothers, wishing on shooting stars,
praying for the roaches to die,
wanting the privacy of my own room
so my breasts could grow in peace.

My diary was my only escape, where I filled
empty pages with experiences I wish I had
until my brothers discovered my secret life,
and I was punished for things I never even did.

Now in the third decade of my life,
whatever child is left in me
pounds on the door to my soul,
pleading to play, but the only game
left for me says
for adults only.

ATLAS

*(earthquake hits San Fernando Valley,
Monday, Jan. 17, 1994. For Salvador).*

He screams in pain,
crushed from the pelvis down,
twenty tons of concrete and steel
on top of one man.

Come pray with me, he strains
as aftershocks shift rubble
and bones.

Rescuers race against time,
nine grueling hours, and
the only difference between life
and death
rests on one man.

THE CLASSROOM
(books that will never be written)

Summer's almost over.
Next week it's back to the classroom
with attitude-filled kids I'll want to kill or kiss -
the know-it-alls, the no-brainers.
I'm not ready for the classroom yet.
Sometimes I wonder if I'll ever be ready.

In the room where the future meets the past
in the present, future leaders and losers listen
to experience, though not all learn. A lot
of times it's me who's learning - learning
what the future really holds. My experiences
are my own - the wisdom I've learned
and try to instill will touch or transform few,
if any.

The innocent faces that stare up at me
are not so innocent anymore,
their innocence either bought or sold or stolen.
Whatever the case, it's innocence near extinction,
kids being shaped for a world that doesn't care
anymore. I wonder if they even care or
if they'll ever care.

Some of the saddest books I've read
are written in their eyes, only
these are the books that will never make it
on the bestseller list.

WHAT I HAVE LEARNED FROM BIRDS

Seagulls. Ravens.
Raspy, raucous voices
making music only gulls and ravens
could love,

and though people call them scavengers,
they're survivors
unlike those pretty birds that sing all day long
and get eaten up by cats.

Somebody has to pick up the trash.

ETERNAL MYSTERY NO. 1

Why is it that you can tickle somebody else,
but you can't tickle yourself?

ONE SUMMER DAY

This silent cemetery
is not so silent today.
The spirits are restless.

Vandals have come
to disturb the dead.
Today, I am unwelcome.

Tombstones, once carved
to last, lay broken
like eggs, spiritual yolk
oozing into the air.

The once friendly breeze
speaks of the unrest
in cold, sacred terms.
Even the flowers wave
at half-mast.

THE FLIGHT

127,000 pounds of metal and flesh
35,000 feet in the air
I am trapped in the belly
of this mechanical bird
I am a modern day Jonah

THE PRICE WE PAY

The equations in life are only part of the answer,
and we all swing on our own axis.
Appled moon, ripe in the sky,
I could take a bite of you,
become my own equation.
Answers are far and few between,
and only in unselfishness
do we find them, but
we are too vain for the simple things
in life.
No fairy tales exist in a sour universe.
We hide within ourselves
wrapped in useless wings.
I want to fly beyond the moon,
safe from the questions,
this knowledge we've inherited.

ASSISTED SUICIDE

Kevorkian is not The Monster,
nor suicide our sister.
Knowledge is not power
as we'd like to think, nor
is it freedom, and
we shall self-destruct in her presence.
What I don't know won't hurt me
as much as what I could know.
I am not ready to die.
Irony has her twisted beauty,
sweetly-coated, no doubt;
her bitterness is not my taste.
Knowledge gives power over others,
but not over the Self.
I choose not to swallow her sallow little pill;
I can die without her help.

WELCOMING THE NEW YEAR MY WAY

7:29 a.m. The New Year is born,
only it doesn't feel like a new year.
Somewhere that feeling died,
but I don't mind anymore,
so I tell myself.

Instead, I embrace the peace I've found
this morning, alone with the sun and
my mug of coffee. Outside a raven perches
atop a naked tree, caws as if it's lost its mate,
then turns and flies away like the years.

I wonder what the new year will bring.
I stopped making resolutions years ago;
they're like bad marriages - they never last.

Across the snow-covered ravine,
the tracks await a distant train,
and if it were warmer, I'd walk down those tracks,
wait for that freight train to thunder by,

count the number of cars, hitch a ride from one
end of town to the other like I did as a child and
pretend I'm going to faraway lands, never to return.

The morning melts away now, anxiety settling
in my bones. I don't want this morning to end
or this year to begin, those damn responsibilities
that keep me from my dreams. Acceptance
is never easy, but somehow I've grown used
to the lines on my face, the wrinkles on my soul,
and the passing of my life
as quickly as a train on New Year's Day.

11

POCKET CHANGE TO LIVE BY

I carry sin in my pockets
in remembrance of you.

You were a butterfly in a dream once,
floating softly with the breeze -

color filled the air
until your wings disappeared.

Life goes on with Sister Time;
I drink the ether in the air

and stumble upon my thoughts.
Where life goes, we'll never know -

so I walk with my hands in my pockets,
the only Truth I know.

THE STORY IN HER EYES

In private, I sit for hours, staring
at a blank computer screen, wishing
all my poetry would flow as easily
as the words of angels and prophets.
Writing would be much easier, and
my visions would bleed in freedom.

My mind fills with images of a young girl
I've only know since September when
she humbly took a seat in my fourth period class -
fuzzy blond hair pulled into a ponytail,
and eyes, beautiful ice blue eyes
I couldn't help but notice, full of questions,
fear, searching for answers that will only come
in time.

She is different from the others,
different because of those eyes
that won't let anyone near.
I've known those eyes before, starving
for something this world can never give.
Sometimes I still see with those eyes.

Worms of hate and suspicion feed
on what's left of her heart, and
I could kill the bastard who put them there.
I want to cut this ridiculous professional line
that separates us, lift her into my heart and
melt the ice around her soul;

and though I'm no angel, no prophet,
I would take her under my wings
with what words I have
and watch her fly.

FOR THE LOVE OF GOD

There are those who take it for granted
that God exists,
and to them, he exists
in a box
or on a crucifix on walls,
around necks,
even in deep pockets
next to lint and loose change
where he is close enough
to be out of the way.

THE OWL

The owl calls out in silent shadows
of crooked trees
'neath an audience of stars,
angels' eyes,

and I, greedy to hear more,
intrude upon its prayer,
thinking not to disarm the alarm
as I threw open my bedroom window,

losing whatever remnants of prayer
lingered before the dawn,
my salvation floating away
on speckled wings.

UNDER CONSTRUCTION

Sitting at my desk, I stare out my window,
pen in hand, never writing a single word
for hours. It's not easy writing poetry.
Sometimes I hate the English language,
especially when I can't think of the precise
words, or grasp the right thoughts,
the foundation of great poems.

Being an English teacher doesn't help.
My mind drifts over some possibles -
the upcoming school year, puppies and
housebreaking, my mother's tomato garden
so ripe and red. There's no logic here today.

Earlier, I had a phone call from a woman I'd hoped
would call. We met at the Viennese Cafe where
she busts her ass as a waitress. A good one.
I was a waitress once. Hated it, until I
took an interest in people. I liked Laura
the moment I met her. She had a certain poetry
about her with her *I Dream of Jeannie* looks, only
prettier, sexier, real.

We had planned a road trip to New Hope today, but
a root canal got the best of her. So, we
rescheduled for Thursday, two days from now.
I hope she doesn't cancel.

I don't know much about her, only that she's a
singer and a songwriter with a Joni Mitchell
influence. She drives a Hyundai which she'd
like to scrap; she volunteers her time at a
wildlife refuge for wounded animals; she's
allergic to penicillin, and her age is a secret.
I'd say my age. I can't tell.

Outside, a new home is under construction,
much like my friendship with Laura. I don't like
to make new friends, but today, for the first time
in years, I want to. I want to tell her things like
a schoolgirl who can't wait to tell her best friend
a big secret. I miss the intimacy of another
woman. My last friend stole my boyfriend, but
that was years ago. I hope they're happy.

Strange how I'm almost nervous about this
Thursday, like it's a first date or something.
It's just that I take great care in building
a friendship, like the crafting of this poem,
or the construction of the new home across
the street, and I'd hate to see this one crumble
before the foundation is even set.

ON THE TOPIC OF DEATH

The rose reaches out in silent fragrance
to those who would know her Mystery.

She needs no face, no scythe, no black cloak.
By Divine Order she does her job,
does it well,

but she would never betray God's secrets,
lest she die
for good.

METAPHOR NO. 1

Regret is a red pen
writing words of shame
on the parchment of the soul.

THINGS THAT BLOOM IN THE NIGHT

Cancer's flower blooms deep
in a once barren womb;
the slow birth of death begins.
She doubles in its grip
like a rubber toy
in the hands of an angry child.

VOLCANO

My dark side shivers
in the Light.

Rage bubbles beneath
my surface.

Demonic holiness damns
me to you.

Pray I don't erupt.

DELUSIO

Cryptic whispers haunt us
in our delusions.
Monsters are real
in such valleys.

Our fears ignite
in raptorial bliss,
and we run awkwardly
in puce shadows.

No one hears
our silent screams
when we imagine
death so near.

Aliens must laugh
at our cowardice,
our primitive existence.
So must the monsters that aren't real.

LIVING IN THE DARK

I'm not comfortable
with the days growing dark
just before 5 pm -
too much darkness for me
to handle anymore.
My life is dark enough.

Somehow over the years,
I've acquired more closet space
than living space -
it's a wonder my skeletons fit at all.

There are times when I'd like to yank
those doors off their hinges,
let the light lick each corner,
expose the truth once and for all,

but I don't want to give myself away
so easily -
I like the secrecy, the darkness
that brings so much color to my life.

THE COST OF FREEDOM

My freedom will cost you your heart,
but I was never yours to begin with.
I came into your life on silent wings
and unspoken prayers because
you were too proud to kneel.
I broke my heart to save yours,
but you refused the wings I gently offered.

a poem for leni b.

he slumps in his seat
in the back of my classroom
eyes bright   cautious
peeking through wavy strands of hair
that would hide his face
if they were long enough

i've seen this mask before
i wore it once
still do at times
when i'm uncomfortable
with myself

he does not know
that he is my personal star
full of passion and savagery
reserved only for angry poets
with nuclear souls and
hearts as far away as Neptune
waiting to be discovered   touched

but he'll never let me tell him this
never believe me   or anyone
as long as he remains eclipsed
by the jealous moon
and if i could change the heavens
i'd erase that moon
give him his own constellation

but no   i'm no galileo
and certainly no god
i'm no one in his personal universe
just a poet passing through
like an unseen comet

POEM ARRIVED AT WHILE FLYING

20,000 feet in the air and climbing.
I swallow to pop my ears
and notice the earth's blanket,
a giant quilt, patches of autumn golds,
squares of cinnamon browns sprinkled
with buttons of trees, all stitched
with ribbons of twisting roads
that hold together a masterful tapestry
designed for humanity.
I didn't know God could sew.

LED ASTRAY

We are wanderers in an ageless dream,
vested with the Curse of Knowledge.

Seek and ye shall find is easier said than done
when we seek to find what science can not give.

We are fish lured by false bait.
Can hunger ever be satisfied?

CROSSROADS

My soul rattles her cage
like a mad mandrill.

The moment of freedom
crashes inside,

and I'm torn at my crossroads
to be perfect.

Failure is a language
we hate to speak.

TRANSFORMATION

I've survived you,
my personal holocaust.
Wicked winters could never
be so cruel.

I've been altered
like a gene, though
no one could ever tell.

I am a Phoenix
ascending from cinders -
I feel Job's power pulsing
in my thin veins.

My personal kingdom
deserves the Light,
so I leave you behind
in your self-dug moat

and crawl
like a victorious leech
from your swamp.
I will not die on your cross.

SAMSARA
(for LJH)

When you die
will you come back
as a mockingbird
at my window?
I'll feed you
every day
as you fill me
with your tireless song.

When I die
I'll come back
as the sun's gentle fingers
all golden and warm -
I'll caress your face
from each day on.
And so our love
shall never die...

SISTER STORM

I pick up her damp scent,
the smell of raw anger.
It won't be long.
Dark clouds squeeze the sun
from its giant window
as thunder rumbles in the throat
of the sky. Ms. Storm begins.
Jagged spears. Wet bullets.
She never misses her mark,
stinging the earth's thirsty skin,
mine if I were there.
I am no stranger to the storm.
We are sisters, and I can feel her anger
as I write. I've studied her anger,
the only passion she's ever known,
so graceful and cruel. She will not
pass unnoticed. Her loneliness
is her anger - it runs in our sisterly blood,
but she'll never know my anger
or the fear, the respect I have for hers.
Sometimes I'm jealous of her beauty,
her power, which is why I wait, hoping
and fearing her departure.
She passes quickly, wringing
her pregnant clouds dry, leaving
her signature smile painted
against her cape of dark clouds,
and so she ends, leaving me
in her wake once again.

JELLO ASS

He pats me like cattle,
making my ass jiggle
like jello out of its mold.
What flavor *am* I?

TREE PEOPLE

Trees are the fingers of the Underworld,
stretching   reaching   for the Light.
Roots grow deep in subconscious soil
hidden from us all.

We are trees in the flesh,
stretching   reaching   for the Light,
our roots somewhere between
the seasons of Heaven and Hell.

FORECLOSURE

A song came on the radio
that I hadn't heard in years -
made me think of my tomboy days
when my brothers were my friends,
and their friends were my friends.
I wondered why I didn't have a penis too.

I was one of the guys -
jumping home-made bike ramps,
skateboarding in no trespassing zones
by the tracks,
climbing dirt mounds and conveyor belts -
a kid's kingdom, where nothing mattered.

Now with our ramps and skateboards gone,
the mounds and belts abandoned,
everything matters
in a kingdom gone up for sale
a long time ago.

FLASHLIGHT TAG IN THE GRAVEYARD

We ran in the darkness
toward the front gates
to escape the light;
one flash and you were it,
a frozen pillar of salt.

I ran over graves,
jumped over stones
to avoid the chase,

and when I tripped
with twisted ankle
into that new deep hole,
the light wasn't quick
enough.

HIBERNATION

Silence calls out
in dark times
when leaves let go
of their limbs
in honor of Winter.

We hide in
our dark caves,
like fat mushrooms,
plump and pale,
unlike the plants of green.

Such distance brings us
closer to ourselves.
Such silence gives us
our Ears to hear.

There are no monsters
in the Dark,
except ourselves
when we are afraid.

Such darkness gives us
the Eyes to see.

CLOSET ANGEL

I found an angel in my closet,
dressed in polka dot pajamas &
when I approached her, she smiled &
asked me if I had an extra pair of wings.
You see, she said, I gave mine up
to help someone else.

WAR BABY
(for Monika)

She stands in my flower bed,
a playground to her,
a flower all her own.

She looks silly in knee pads
and gloves, an array of garden tools
at her feet.

She fills a bucket with water
and Miracle Gro, stirs, then pours
her magic into these yawning beds.

She explains each plant to me -
weeds, ferns, azalea bushes, rhododendrons -
all dead, and hollers at my neglect, my ignorance.

She transforms my yard into a humble eden
in a matter of hours, using every single minute
of sunlight as if it were her last, and makes me
promise to water each night until each flower
is rooted. I promise.

With this promise, I secretly vow to watch
each leaf, each petal unfold in beauty,
in purity just as I've watched her unfold
over the years.

Sometimes I see our roles reversing;
lately she's the child, and I'm the parent
even though I have no children of my own.

She is a war baby
left over from the aftermath of Hitler,
left to survive, to remember

the simplicity and the innocence
stolen from her as a child in Nuremburg.

She tends to each plant with precise care,
and as I watch, I can't imagine how she survived
the bombing of her home, all her treasures burning
as she stood watching, flames reflecting
in her eyes.

I can't imagine the fear that singed her soul
each time the air raid sirens wailed, then
desperately running for safety, for life,
to an underground shelter for days at a time
until the raids passed.

I can't imagine her hopes when her grandfather
waved a dirty white sheet as a flag from the bunker
only to see those hopes turn into horror
when someone shot him anyway.

I can't imagine the hunger she felt, never
knowing when her next meal would be, living
in constant fear and filth, sleeping on cold
metal bunks and straw mats with only her
dreams keeping her alive.

I can't imagine her bitterness,
abandoned by a soldier for a father,
neglected by a young whore for a mother,
given to an orphanage filled with other
forgotten children;

and so it always amazes me,
even after all these years, how she eats
a chicken wing, devouring it as if it were her last
meal, sucking the very marrow from the bones,
leaving each one empty, clean, and free,

an art I'll never understand.

The sun is almost gone now
except for the few rays that make her glow
before me like never before.
She is more beautiful than any flower,
standing in this sanctuary she's created,
standing like a warrior in her knee pads,
dirt-caked gloves and clothes, wisps of hair
hanging in her glowing, sweating face.

She is a war baby for sure, surviving
more than I could ever endure.
I wish I could give her everything
that was stolen from her;
I wish I could be her mother,
but she's too strong for that,

and it makes me feel sad to know that I, too,
have neglected the little things
that are so important to her,
like a flower garden,
which is why she hands me her bucket
of water and Miracle Gro, her legacy,
and tells me without words
that it's time to learn all over again.

EDUCATION

Summer's close. I can finally forget
the teacher in me, yank out the child
squirming within, craving to play in nature,
my classroom. Adventure, travel, challenges
that make me sweat, work hard, appreciate life.
I want to live simply this summer, trade my
suitcases for a backpack and a tent, carry
only what I need to survive, and sleep
under the stars. I want to climb Kilimanjaro's
giant face, acquaint myself with Kenyan culture,
and dance under the sun with painted natives.
I want to descend the Sun Kosi in Nepal in
a paddle boat, trek through the Solo Khumbu
region. I want to visit Buddhist temples and
chant with the monks, commune with my Maker.
I want to meander through small, remote villages,
buy things at the Ramjartar bazaar. I want to
acclimatize to the altitude in La Paz and visit
Tiwanaku before heading into the Cordillera Real.
I want to hunt antelope with tribesmen and their
women, learn their tongue, their primitive ways,
pierce my nose and become part of them.
Let this summer season my life with the spices
of these other worlds. Let me live dangerously,
free, the way God meant me to live, bring my
karma full circle for the first time in my life
and come home the teacher I'm meant to be.

41

JUSTICE

Somewhere in the night
a vigilante cries to his gods,
his demons.

Pain is too organic at times.

THE END

The Storm passes quietly
like a mermaid in the Night.
The ocean breeze whispers
Secrets from the Deep.

I slip into phantasmal oblivion,
riding rainbows and unknown dreams.
Angels swoop sericeously to guide
my questioning soul home
to newfound freedom.

Whispers lure me
through labyrinths of time
where only timelessness
exists.

I pass the Setting Sun
beyond gates of children and poets.
An albatross flies ahead
and Freedom wraps her chilly shawl
around my accepting shoulders
while my earthly cradle
awaits completion.

CRAVINGS

The sweet tooth within
craves a subtle afternoon

surrounded by friendly strangers
and cafes and the *cloppity clop*

of hooves on cobblestone streets,
the sun dancing in her bright yellow suit,

making flowers smile and lovers toast
in pure oblivion to all around.

A dream of a distant time perhaps,
but I live it in my mind

like a soul searching
for an opening to the Womb.

REINCARNATION

Leagues of angels cross boundaries
of time, space, and souls
when miracles are scheduled for birth.
Spiritual surgery needs no medicine.

Life doesn't offer guarantees,
and emptiness is only temporary silence,
a division we suffer within our Soul.

Our existence is not so pure,
yet we spend our lives
in the hell of purification.
Perfection has her price.

HYENAS ON WELFARE

nocturnal carnivores
animal kingdom scum
scavengers of carrion
enemies to the King
stalking and sneaking
stealing what doesn't belong
always taking
never giving
always circling and circling
like a pack of mad vampires -
get a real job

ON TOUR

Spring kisses the sycamore
outside my two story window.
Armlike branches stretch
after a long wintry sleep.
Manicured fingers of green
point toward the sun -
it's an invitation to magic.

The ravens come,
inviting themselves
without any shame.
Six caw in chorus;
a rainbow of music resounds.

There is no dissonance
when Spring conducts her symphony -
and when the ravens finish,
they flutter away,
leaving the branches to click
in ovation.

ROYALTY

The Royal Family remains eclipsed.
Adultery. Divorce. Scandal.
Truth will always breed in closets
until there is no more room.
We are created equal,
so the Law goes.
All blood carries sin,
our link to any throne.

AN EYE FOR AN EYE
(on the scheduled executions of
Billy Bailey & John Taylor)

One man wears a rope necklace;
another sits in a chair custom-built
to collect his blood.

They have no choice but
to give their lives
for the one Commandment
they chose to break.

Justice must wear a blindfold
because she knows Truth's
ugly side.

Medieval? Barbaric?
Who said Justice has to be humane?

CHOICE

Carnal pleasures guide us to false freedoms
like the Snake to tempting fruit.
Subtlety is camouflaged cruelty,
a joke on our kind;
that which tempts us becomes our poison.
We do not keep our personal devils at bay
especially when they appear like angels
offering vacuous temples
for our easily misguided souls.
This soul can't afford another mortgage.

THE GAME

A football legend falls short of the goal,
face-masked by society.
Whatever lesson he must learn
will not be an easy one to score;
it's certainly not ours,

but victory will only be his
once Job flows through his veins.
Divine challenges are never easy,
and pride before any Fall
is the hot spice used to bring out

the real flavor of any man.
Yet we still spectate
in one man's game,
shouting like critics.
What if the ball were in our hands?

SO CLOSE, SO FAR

The moon brings no satisfaction
to hungry souls or tired dancers,

nor does it cast a witch's magic for her,
yet we embrace the illusion

like secret lovers in search
of a cool, refreshing breeze.

Deception lies closer to the Truth
than Truth itself.

IRRECONCILABLE DIFFERENCES

I see the difference -
two mental moons.
Your world is your own.

Alive in your trenches,
you swallow your fear
in fatal does.
Your war is within.

I am no personal jesus.
Do not cling to me -
I have my own crutches,
my own crosses to bare.

Leave me in Silence and
go find your own.
You seek a rainbow
I cannot give.

FLOWER ANGEL

Angels bloom everywhere.
Once I met one on my way to work &
she told me that the stars
were really heaven's flowers &
I said how come they don't smell like flowers &
she said you can only smell them
once you pick them with your soul.

SAYING GOODBYE

Last night a dream pulled me
back to my roots when my father
said goodbye, leaving
part of his life behind
to start a new one.

He was happy, younger than I remember;
and I was a child waving
with a tear in my eye, wishing
I could go with him, but

realizing the apron strings were cut
long before they were ever tied.
I've watched my father change through the years,
growing older and younger at the same time,

if that's possible -
changes I've grown to accept, even though
I wasn't part of them, making
me feel like an outsider

more than a daughter at times -
I've often wondered if he feels the same.
Now, as I look at his perfect blue eyes,
I see he is ready, the dream true.

The child within me cries tears
full of the things we could have shared,
tears I've always wanted to cry
but couldn't.

ODE TO A CHRISTMAS TREE ON WILSON LAKE

The rain drizzles to a stop
as the fog lifts her damp veil,
revealing a wet New Year.

The lake's pulse is calm
and thick with mud
until a lone mallard stirs
its coffee surface.

On the deck, two men heave the stripped tree
onto the rocks below
where it is stopped by a sister tree.
She fares well
except for her broken top,
a fallen crown.

Remnants of sprayed flakes
float languorously in the aftermath
like spirits after a senseless tragedy.
They too will settle.

little girl poem no. 1

little girl   scared
hides under kitchen table
parents fighting   again
father yells
calls her mother a slut
hits her hard   into the wall
mother screams   kicks
wipes blood from her chin
as a cockroach scuttles
across the tiled floor
little girl run
run like your brother
cry for your mother
fight like jesus
last chance last chance
before your soul becomes a ghetto

PURGATORY

We live with our heads in heaven,
walk with our feet in hell.
There is no in between
except the purgatory
in our hearts.

GEOMETRY

Prepare for landing from 35,000 feet.
My stomach rises into my throat.
How fast can a plane fall out of the sky?
(I'd rather not know).

The metal bird rumbles, rocking slightly.
(This is the first time I didn't have to pop
my ears).
Geometry from this angle is beautiful.
15,000 more feet and I, too,
will be part of the equation.

execution style

my husband says i'm a real sick bitch
says my words are too graphic
says my tongue is as blunt as a bayonet
says i'm more dangerous than a bullet
says i can wake a dead man
says i cut through the soul
says i should be an executioner
rather than a poet
pullin' the switch would be easy

INNOCENCE LOST

Sitting on a midnight beach,
I stare at the bone-white moon
with its tilted face.
Such a jealous moon, robbing
rich colors from my sight.

My mind meanders through streams of thoughts,
memories I wish I could forget, people
I should forgive, but I can still smell
his hot, drunken breath, feel it on my skin,
his hungry hands groping in places I promised
I'd keep pure until I married.

He was old enough to be my father.
I wince at the thought of being a statistic -
such a harsh, apropos word for someone
who's become both fragile and hardened since
then. But I don't cry or call myself a victim
anymore.

Above, the moon whispers my name,
and I wonder how she survives
the loneliness of time and space,
no life to give or take, except
the color she steals from the world tonight,
much like the innocence I lost.

THE HUNTING LODGE

Seven dead deer
hang on a rack

by their hind feet
as prize trophies

in a game they
never entered.

THE TREE
(for LJH)

A tree stands alone;
its trunk twists along the ground,
inviting us to sit in its lap.
This is the perfect place for a picnic.

Around us, the tall grass sways
to the music of the wind.
We remain the steady note.

I reach to touch your hand
that has grown strong
over the years like the trunk
of this tree,

and like this tree, our love
remains solid and alive
despite the storms that come.

The tree raises its thick arms
in praise. I place my arms
around your body as a sigh
escapes my soul, knowing
why the birds rest here.

PELICANS

Pelicans do not know they're ugly.
We do not know their beauty,
and so transcendence begins.

The pelican flies free
and precise,
inches above the curling sea,
scooping fishes like faith.

INVASION

Psychic bombardment.
I smell the moon at work.
I know you're alive
lurking on the outskirts
of my mind.

I could invite you in -
then tilt my plane,
watch you slide
away
into holy abyss -
my illegal alien.

THOUGHTS ABOUT EASTER

The sun breaks through
a thick ceiling of clouds
on this Holy Thursday,
and I have off until Tuesday,

thank God,
from twittering student
who'd rather have sex or get stoned
than study English.

Yeah, Easter is here.
Soon, this weekend will fill
with phony festivities -
kids hunting for colored eggs

they'll never eat,
people attending church
for the first time in a year
(as if this will save them).

Jesus is secondary,
secondary to a long-eared,
bucked-tooth rodent named Peter
that lays eggs. Whatever.

MCDANIEL'S PRINCIPLES

1. Never hate your enemies. You may need their help one day, and you may even become good friends.

2. If someone needs help, help. You could find yourself in need someday.

3. Satisfy your cravings and you'll find you'll have them less. It's your body's way of saying it deserves good things.

4. Working out is good for you. It's a year-round commitment. When you have your health, you have everything.

5. Always, always laugh at yourself. We're human; we make mistakes. Without our mistakes, we could never appreciate success. We are, thank God, *not* perfect in every way.

6. Don't follow footsteps. Make your own.

7. Smile! It's the only thing understood in every language. If you see someone without a smile, give him one of yours. It takes more muscles in your face to frown than to smile.

8. Never take life too seriously. Life is meant to be lived, not planned. Take life one day at a time - it's the only way it's given to us, and it's the only way we can spend it.

9. Always tell the truth, even if it hurts. The problem with lying is that you have to remember your lies.

67

10. Always forgive yourself and others.
Forgiveness is the highest degree of love. If God is
big enough to forgive and forget our sins, who are
we to remember?

11. If you're expecting your ship to come in, don't
hang around the airport or bus station.

12. Change is good, no matter how much it hurts
or how bad it seems. Change means you're being
pushed in the right direction. Never, never, never
give up on yourself.

13. Always take time to remember the beautiful
and the simple things in life. And always give your
thanks because you'll never know when those
things, or people, will be taken away from you.

THE MERMAID
(for LF)

She clings to a silent rock
in a distant ocean all her own,
singing a lonely lament
no one has ever heard
except the crescent moon.

The jagged reef imprisons her
in its gigantic mouth, making
navigation impossible,
for surely those who dare
only die.

Beautiful to gaze upon,
dangerous to approach,
and with a splash
she's gone.

MUTINY ON THE BOUNTY
(a sonnet)

O Pirate! Thou hast looted my very Jewel!
Captured and ravished, upon a great Vessel I rode!
Swashbuckler! Savage! A man ever so cruel!
A man of Desire and Passion, in Heaven I strode!
Come back to me, Master! I cry to the air,
For thou hast bound me with Passion, unleased my Soul.
From the Plank to the Deep, I soon shall despair
Should thou not return quickly else Love taketh its toll.
Time floateth in endless waves; I relive crimes of the heart
With thy naked figure burning as embers in my mind.
Do ever my thoughts light upon thy Soul's secret parts?
O Mutiny! How they absence leaveth me part blind!
    May Time never teach me what I refuse to learn,
    Without my heart's Captain, I have nothing to yearn.

LOOKING AT OURSELVES

Life.
A generous gift
with too many consequences
when opened.
We do not know
what we want,
who we are,
who we aren't.
We travel in endless
circles like a hurricane,
defining ourselves
through others' eyes
with accurate imperfection.
We are mirrors
for one another,
yet we do not look
at such reflections.

THOUGHTS ON EXCELLENCE

Darkness lurks
on the edge
of our souls -
an abyss designed
to complement the Light.
We create
our own inner boundaries,
selfish and cruel.
Excellence doesn't
make us perfect.

HOPE

Butterflies congregate at my old window,
bringing me a new world of light.

Freedom throws its life preserver my way,
but I am a castaway, black sheep deluxe.

My brass ring is styrofoam -
will it carry my weight?

THE HOMESTRETCH

Some say over the hill
means the end is near,
the goal is in sight,
the journey almost done.

I have seen many hills
in my quiet life, foothills,
mountains, especially
the valleys in between.

I follow the sun each day
of my journey, making sure
not to rush the moment -
or miss the smiles of flowers,

the invitations of trees,
the private performance of a
mockingbird silhouetted
against the setting sun.

In the evening, when stars
become the eyes of angels,
I curl like a kitten and dream
dreams at the foot of God.

I know my time will come -
my body will give up its ghost
so that another may live
to journey as I have,

and I shall fly high above the hills,
the mountains, the valleys in between,
dipping now and then.

BURIAL

Bury me under the harvest moon
deep in October
beyond a great forest -
tuck me into the earth's womb,
sprinkle me with pear seeds -
I wanna grow my own tree
filled with unspoken words -
roots will spread their gnarled fingers
through my forgotten ribs, and
when my golden fruit ripens,
taste me -
I too shall give life.

SIDE ROAD IN ALABAMA ON A DECEMBER MORNING

Today I learned mistletoe is a parasite,
a tree its host,
an odd thing for a father
to teach his daughter
on a late morning drive.

Then, everywhere I looked
trees blossomed with this beautiful virus -
I thought of its power to make people kiss
and how contagious beauty really is.

DIVISION

Beyond emotional boundaries
there is no horizon,
no pots of gold,
no rainbows.

We cater to the Self
at such boundaries
where the flower is raped
repeatedly
of its nectar.

The flower gives.
The thief steals.
It is the state of grace
that divides.

SUNSET ON THE GULF

The days grow shorter,
sunlight fades into majestic purple,
brilliant orange. The death
of another day.

The sun dips below the eye's
horizon; its afterglow lingers,
illuminating two dolphins,
probably mates, on their way
to everywhere.

The beach is empty, quiet,
except for the lapping of
tiny waves, the ocean's
heartbeat.

Two lovers hold hands,
invoking a oneness separate
from the rest of the world.
She rests her head on his
shoulder, he gently kisses
her forehead, brushes away
a strand of dancing hair.

The dolphins slip in and out,
unafraid it seems of what rests
below or ahead, oblivious
to what's behind and the lovers
who salute in return.

POETRY IN MOTION

Universe. One Verse.
A giant poem written by God.
no beginning   no end
Existing because it exists.
Interpretation restricts.
Condemnation rejects.
There is no science
in the breath of God.

FLATWOODS CEMETERY

Decoration Day will visit Flatwoods soon,
when relatives from Jersey, Michigan, and Bama
breathe life into this old graveyard,
resurrecting its past once again.

The tall whispering weeds will be pulled
by loving hands and replaced with fresh flowers
and wreaths. The silent church bells will ring
again throughout this forgotten town.

Dad will stand over his father's grave
and tell the same old stories:
his daddy's bootlegging days,
his son's untimely death,
his uncle's death in Normandy,
his brother's drinking and cancer -
will they ever get any rest?

Kids will giggle, playing hide-and-seek
among the stones, and I'll meet relatives
I never knew I had. Once I met a man
I could have fallen in love with, but
he turned out to be an uncle's cousin's son,
something like that.

The old southern cemetery stands silent,
its stones like chess pieces in a stalemated game.
Such a beautiful graveyard, though
it's only decorations are these words.

MORNING

The sun rises,
shedding a blanket
of clouds - golden
streaks burst
like fingers jolted
with life.

You lie next to me,
curled like a fetus -
you've not returned
from the deep. Your
rib cage rises
falls
rises
falls
in slow, gentle rhythm.

I spoon myself around
you and your dreams,
synchronize my breathing
with yours, careful
not to wake you.

The sun's fingers penetrate
the room - you stir slightly
under her warm touch, then
stretch with the grace of a cat
before I receive you into
my life once again.

homicidal tendencies

it would be easy to kill you
easier than writing poetry
i'd kill you without a conscience
make you pay for all your accusations
hurting me over and over and over

i could damage! damage! damage!
be the madwoman i crave to be
pour my wrath out on innocent victims
choke the very life out of them
one by one   and get off on it
yeah...make them feel my pain
my power   and think of you to the very
last breath

some game you play
always pushin' away the ones that love you
hate you   because you can't handle love

i'd eat your pumping heart right out of your chest
let the blood drip from my chin to my hands
i'd paint my face with it   decorate the warrior
in me   let your blood dry and crack
all over my body

then step   into the shower   and just
let
   you
      drain
            away...

DESERT FRUIT

The apple takes the blame
for a crime it did not commit,
and so it bares the red skin of shame.

Eden is a desert now,
unholy and fruitless;
such absence allows devils
to run free.

The desert is not friendly -
any life would be a miracle
whether a cactus or scorpion.

Its world stings us with illusions;
what we think is real
could never survive her heat;

and so our dreams disappear in tiny waves
when we reach outside ourselves like
apples without cores.

RESCUING SALVATION: A LESSON IN TOUGH LOVE

I am not afraid of you,
my Dark Thorn.
I am not afraid of the temptation
anymore.
Your kind of love is not love,
not love,
though you see it as such.

Subtle traps snare
transitional souls -
illusion becomes reality
for unprepared desertwalkers.
Only fools know selfish desires.

No, I am not afraid of you,
my Dark Thorn.
I am not afraid of you
anymore.
I pluck you from my heart
to become a Garden on your own -
it's the only love I know.

LISTENING TO WIND CHIMES ON GROUND HOG'S DAY

Chimes sweep soft sounds into my soul,
touching areas reserved only
for secrets and dreams.

Ancient books line the shelves
of this quiet bookstore, biding time
as I sometimes do.

Auras connect in sandalwood
incense. Smoke rises like a genie,
mistress to selfish wishes.

A small fountain trickles.
Coins tossed by wish seekers
project surreal images

found only in dreams and hallucinations,
creating a world of illusions
and wishes that may never come true.

I could float in this fountain,
let it soothe my tired soul
(if it could hold this soul);

I'd float away into a timeless dream,
reclaim the youth I once had
but could never enjoy.

Another wish sinks silently
to the bottom...
a thread of loneliness

tugs at the fabric of my soul,
pulling me back to a reality
that could never be wished away.

little girl poem no. 2

girl   your daddy's drunk again
whatcha gonna do?
your momma's achin' in a hospital bed
broken ribs   bloodied soul
told the doctor she fell down the stairs
last time it was a ladder
girl   your momma's runnin' out of excuses
whatcha gonna do?

one of those pretty birds is singing
outside your bedroom window
makes you cry 'cause you're not free
like them
girl   your daddy's got an ulcer for a soul
he don't care no more
tiltin' that bottle into that hole in his face
makes you wish it was the barrel of a gun
your finger pullin' the trigger

girl   you sun is goin' down fast
and your pretty bird has stopped its singin'
take that drug of numbness girl
'cause there ain't nothin' you can do

CURSED

We come into this world
void of spirit
but full of innocence
that's easier to steal.

Life offers no guarantees
and the future never reveals herself
when we want her to. She's a hidden
bride to us all.

Once our innocence is seasoned
and fattened for the kill,
we become our own sacrificial lambs
wanting more than life can offer.

Greed is our only flaw,
honey with a sting -
one taste
and the slaughter begins.

MARKETING

A harem of flowers unfolds its truth,
spilling perfume in boldness and grace.

Along comes the bee,
the perfect victim -
even Nature sets her traps.

THE GRAVEYARD

I walk naked among century old stones
when I want nature on my side.
I let the summer sun bathe me
in her cup of ambrosial rays,
and like a lizard with jeweled eyes,
I bask lazily
upon Eliza's quiet, pine-needled grave
as flowers lend their sweet perfume,
luring my nose more closely
to their fragrant faces,
tiny petals smiling
with the rosy innocence of cherubs.
A butterfly floats by
on the whispers of saints,
lands on my hand, a momentary altar,
then flies upward like a prayer,
the price of communion a soul.

TODAY'S EXHIBIT

The surf awakens. No moon to greet me
or tempt me, just the early morning sun
yawning in a tangerine sky, gently kissing
the night goodbye, making me feel the passage
of time.

My past is a world of colors run dry,
leaving memories painted on the canvas
of my mind - memories fading in the gallery
of my soul, a museum of time when each memory
was worth a novel of words.

I remember when magic permeated the air,
and I was as invincible as God -
nothing was impossible, but somewhere
something changed, and I became vulnerable
like everyone else,

living in a world where responsibilities
and restrictions shroud that magic,
making it disappear. Sometimes
I'd like to disappear.

I was the princess of this beach once,
running from pillaging pirates,
hiding behind soft dunes
among unsuspecting lovers -
I always escaped.

Now the sun rises to her power,
triumphant over the night;
and I must forget the princess,
lock her away, for now,
from a world she could never escape.

murderess

somewhere in my universe
she stands erect
unmovable
no vision
no despair
no pain
a woman of stone
unable to see
or do
or think
or even feel

somewhere in my dead universe
i really am alive
like a silent killer
i must hold myself together
unlike this skin that i make bleed

i am a puzzle even to myself
and i hold each piece
in hardening hands
i will not put these pieces together
i might find out who i am

METAPHOR NO. 2

Frustration.
A steel pair
of handcuffs
imprisoning
one within
his own soul.

SEEING THE RAIN

Another rainy day in November.
When I was a kid growing up
on the other side of the tracks
where the other poor kids lived,
I believed rain was the tears
of angels who felt sorry for us,
but I've outgrown that philosophy,
I think.

I remember playing in summer rains
when our idea of a built-in pool
was the flooded field down the block,
when doing rain dances kept
the angels crying so our pool wouldn't empty,
when cars would splash us while we stood
pointing at large puddles on the side of the road,
our wet playground.

Life was simple then. Carefree. Magical.
We could turn anything into a playground -
garbage dumps for King of the Mountain,
graveyards for Flashlight Tag,
gravel pits for streaking - our possibilities
and curiosity were endless.

The rain is slowing now.
Above, clouds separate, drift away,
making me sad. The child within
doesn't want the rain to end,
or the magic I've been feeling
for these few brief moments.
Maybe, just maybe, if I look up
I might even see an angel
wiping the tears from her face.

DECISIONS

Invisible boundaries
create conflict
in the Soul, leaving
no room to run free
or play.

Decisions start in hell,
private and raw.

No god will answer.
No guru will guide.
Let me put this knowledge
up for sale.

THE FALL

An angel hides his face in shame
beneath his clipped wings -
the price of knowledge was too much.
Shame is the poison we all taste.

VAMPIRES

Interview With The Vampire
explodes in theaters everywhere.
Crowds clot the lobby
to quench their own greedy thirst.
We are no different.

ONE PARTICULAR MOMENT

He called me Patty O'Malley
even though that wasn't my name,
as he stood at the mike
before a crowd of 40some people -
musicians, storytellers, poets,
gathered for celebration,
sharing the gift of creativity,
every moment counting
in the upper room
of the Friends Meeting House.

His name was Eric Federov,
a big man with an even bigger soul,
a brother of the arts, the spoken word.
He spoke of reflection and truths so simple
they're often overlooked,

but not by a poet, the Midas of words,
giving things life, if only briefly.
When Eric finished, he called me Patty again.
I smiled as a poet would.

TO A BROAD STREET DOG ON APRIL FOOL'S DAY

Yesterday I saw you
barking at passers-by,
letting them know

you were boss
with your raggedy-assed coat
and high-pitched bark.

You didn't scare me.
I chuckled and
thought of my dog,

always barking and growling,
acting tough. You'd
probably run

if I barked back.
You owned your little world,
never letting anyone near.

But, today the world
bought you, and I cried
when I saw you on the side

of the road, my smile
u-turning. You scared me,
scared me for the first time -

blood dripping from your small,
spotted face.
I was as helpless

as you. I swallow this lump
in my throat, knowing
that this world owns me too.

MIDSUMMER TEACHER BLUES

On the brink of autumn,
the new school year,
reality kicks in,
shifting us into gear.

We open a briefcase,
rummage through old lesson plans,
faded answer keys, papers we somehow
forgot to grade, students' drawings
and poems saying *goodbye,*
we'll visit next year,

and a favorite pen next to the
watergun we forgot to return,
and realize, again, that blue
is the color of our summer.

FLYING LESSON NO.1

I rise from the grave,
free from corporeal Self,
my wings wet with dew.

Today I shall learn to fly
in silent rhythm -
this nest has no more eggs.

My wing tips shall span galaxies,
heaven and hell, life and death.

You shall know me by my Eagle heart,
and I will make my nest among the stars.

A POEM THAT DOESN'T MATTER

In a hollow world,
we are strangers to ourselves,
our paths clouded by mist and rules.

I could hold the moon in my hand
if I so wanted, but
that would be too practical
for you;

throwing miracles your way
involves too much science,
and when all is said and done,
this poem won't even matter.

ON HOLY GROUND

I sit on deserted chapel steps,
dress undone,
nakedness exposed
like the day I was born.

My womanhood has freed
itself from your chains,
and now I must cleanse
myself of the devils
you once injected into me.
I fell from grace
like a rebellious angel
when I let you touch
my wings.

Like a vampire in need
of native soil, I come
to holy ground to bury
memories, demons
that haunt me,
to resurrect whatever holiness
is left in me, though it's hard to fly
with broken wings.

THE FIGHT

The doubt begins.
Anger gnaws the soul
like anxious devils.
Accusations explode
into violence,
a virus now loose.
Down she goes,
a paper doll
at your disposal.

PILLOW ANGEL

An angel stopped me in a dream &
asked me if she could rest within my Soul.
She said she had been working overtime &
needed a place to stay & I told her
I had no pillow to rest her weary wings &
she said that's OK, I'll just use your heart.

THE DEATH PENALTY

Truth is not all wild flowers
and rainbows of promise.
Sometimes she must show
her ugly side.

Death is the black sheep
in Truth's family, and
sometimes she must spin
her dark wool in honor of Justice.

Why else is a judge's robe black?

CHALLENGER 7
(on the anniversary)

All in the name of Science,
a crew dies minutes after take-off.

The Universe needs a much
bigger cage.

ONE

I bleed in unison
with Nature's pulse.
We are one -
but she lives freely
outside the confines
of a body and
because of this,
she'll never bleed.
Lucky her.
Our heartbeat is
the presence of God
though we live forever -
separately - the same word,
different meanings.

SANCTIONS

Children with turgid abdomens
exist in Man's wasteland,
their only hope lying
in the thing that destroys them.

FAIR GAME

Salute the sinner
who's seen and done all -
all in the name of Self.
The world is not safe
for some.

Tune in,
my starstruck friend -
tell the sinner
about the fairness
of the universe.

Isn't there something
you'd like to do?
Breaking free is easy
once you break yourself.

See the sinner dance
alive in a dead world.
He is fair to himself,
true to his nature.

Sin is a game
we are born and
bred to play.
How fair is that?

STRIKING DISTANCE

i've been writing this stuff
for years
because no one would ever
listen -
i know i can get away
with it.

beware the silent children
who reach
their breaking point just out of
view -
they know when no one's
looking.

VALLEY FORGE

I sit on a stone wall
high above the Schuylkill River.
Dusk begins to settle.

It is in this silence
that I hear the voices -
soldiers of the Revolution,
the screams, the prayers.

The snap of a twig
catches my attention -
deer surround me,
watching, waiting,
antlers raised like guns.

TEMPEST

I see past your ignorance.
And though I am not black
or yellow or red,
I might as well be in your eyes.

Like a witch I burn
in your judgment,
but I will not betray
my truth, no matter the cost.

Tie me to your stake,
release me of this flesh -
I shall vomit devils
from the grave.

My ghost will feed
upon your children
and your children's children;
they will lift me in prayer and song;
my spirit shall rise
above your shadow.

I will bring storms to your soul,
earthquakes to your spirit -
and when your pride swallows
you whole, remember Jonah,
remember Moses, remember
Judas and Jesus. Remember
what it takes to make a rainbow.

from one poet to another
(for rdf)

you once wrote me poetry
filled with moonlight and love
we thought would last
forever -
we were innocent enough
to think so, but
like pressed flowers
in some forgotten novel,
those words faded
like the face of the moon
in the morning sun.

we hid in your parents' trailer,
making love in cramped teenage style,
stealing moments whenever we could -
and when your dad knocked,
we scattered
like two cockroaches,
ashamed of our deed,
of loving too much.

HELL FOR A KNOW-IT-ALL

Had a dream
where Lucifer was Jesus' twin brother.
Identical.
Long hair, beard, eyes that just pull
your soul in.
At one point, I couldn't tell
who was who
and I got scared, thinking,
how would I possibly choose
between these two simply by looking
at them, especially if my salvation,
my eternity, depended on my choice?
Neither would give me a straight answer
if I asked. Jesus would speak a parable.
Lucifer would talk in twisted terms.
Poor Eve, she had no clue.

INDEX OF FIRST LINES

INDEX OF FIRST LINES

INDEX OF FIRST LINES

INDEX OF FIRST LINES

INDEX OF FIRST LINES

INDEX OF TITLES

INDEX OF TITLES

ORDER FORM

* Telephone orders: Call 1(610) 933-9462.

* On-line orders: E-mail WARBABY96@aol.com

* Postal orders: Hasor-Plenny Publishing
                  Suite 47
                  1220 Valley Forge Road
                  P.O. Box 987
                  Valley Forge, PA 19482-0987

Payment:
Send $9.95 check or money order payable to
Hasor-Plenny Publishing.

****

Please send me _____ copies of **WAR BABY** to:

Name:_____

Company:_____

Address:_____

City:_____

State:_____ _____Zip:_____

Telephone:(_____)_____

ORDER FORM

* Telephone orders: Call 1(610) 933-9462.

* On-line orders: E-mail WARBABY96@aol.com

* Postal orders: Hasor-Plenny Publishing
                  Suite 47
                  1220 Valley Forge Road
                  P.O. Box 987
                  Valley Forge, PA 19482-0987

Payment:
Send $9.95 check or money order payable to
Hasor-Plenny Publishing.

****

Please send me _____ copies of WAR BABY to:

Name:_____

Company:_____

Address:_____

City:_____

State:_____Zip:_____

Telephone:(_____)_____

ORDER FORM

* Telephone orders: Call 1(610) 933-9462.

* On-line orders: E-mail WARBABY96@aol.com

* Postal orders: Hasor-Plenny Publishing
                  Suite 47
                  1220 Valley Forge Road
                  P.O. Box 987
                  Valley Forge, PA 19482-0987

Payment:
Send $9.95 check or money order payable to
Hasor-Plenny Publishing.

****

Please send me _____ copies of WAR BABY to:

Name:_____

Company:_____

Address:_____

City:_____

State:_____Zip:_____

Telephone:(_____)_____